LST

IN THE DESERT OF DREAD

TRACEY TURNER

Crabtree Publishing Company

Crabtree Publishing Company
www.crabtreebooks.com
1-800-387-7650

616 Welland Ave.
St. Catharines, ON
L2M 5V6

PMB 59051, 350 Fifth Ave.
59th Floor,
New York, NY

Published by Crabtree Publishing Company in 2015.

Author: Tracey Turner

Illustrator: Nelson Evergreen

Project coordinator: Kelly Spence

Editor: Alex Van Tol, Kathy Middleton

Proofreader: Wendy Scavuzzo

Prepress technician: Ken Wright

Print and Production coordinator:
Katherine Berti

Text copyright © 2014 Tracey Turner

Illustration copyright © 2014 Nelson Evergreen

Copyright © 2014 A & C Black

Additional images © Shutterstock

WARNING!
The instructions in this book are for extreme
survival situations only. Always proceed with
caution, and ask an adult to supervise—or, if
possible, seek expert help. If in doubt, consult a
responsible adult.

Printed in Canada/102014/EF20140925

Library and Archives Canada
Cataloguing in Publication

Turner, Tracey, author
    Lost in the desert of dread / Tracey Turner.

(Lost : can you survive?)
Includes index.
ISBN 978-0-7787-0725-7 (bound).--
ISBN 978-0-7787-0733-2 (pbk.)

    1. Plot-your-own stories. I. Title.

PZ7.T883Lo 2014   j823'.92
C2014-904010-5

Library of Congress
Cataloging-in-Publication Data

Turner, Tracey.

  Lost in the desert of dread / by Tracey Turner ;
illustration, Nelson Evergreen. -- American edition.
    pages cm. -- (Lost: can you survive?)
  Includes index.
  ISBN 978-0-7787-0725-7 (reinforced library
binding) -- ISBN 978-0-7787-0733-2 (pbk.)
  1. Plot-your-own stories. [1. Deserts--Fiction. 2.
Survival--Fiction. 3. Sahara--Fiction. 4. Plot-
your-own stories.] I. Evergreen, Nelson, 1971-
illustrator. II. Title.

  PZ7.T8585Lom 2014
  [Fic]--dc23
                      2014022785

Contents

5 Map of Africa

6 Welcome to your adventure!

10 Desert Survival Tips

15 Jackals

16 Heatstroke

19 Deathstalker Scorpions

23 Shelter in the Desert

25 Hyponatremia

27 Adapting for the Desert

29 Making a Fire in the Desert

33 Saw-scaled Vipers

37 Using a Watch as a Compass

41 Spotted Hyenas

43 Sandstorms

46 Dysentery

49 Desert Wells and Water Holes

55 Edible Desert Plants

57 Parasite-borne Diseases

59 Sand Cats

65 Sand Dunes

67 Ostriches

69 Desert Gourds

71 Making a Solar Still

77 Flash Floods

79 Quicksand

81 Keeping Hydrated

85 Rain in the Desert

91 Baboons

95 Mirages

· 97 Camels

101 Solpugids

107 Barbary Sheep

115 Oases

116 The People of the Sahara Desert

117 Sahara Mountains

117 Expanding Sahara

118 Other Deserts

119 How much water do you need to drink?

120 Real-life Lost-in-the-Desert Stories

122 Glossary

124 Learning More

125 Websites

126 Index

Africa

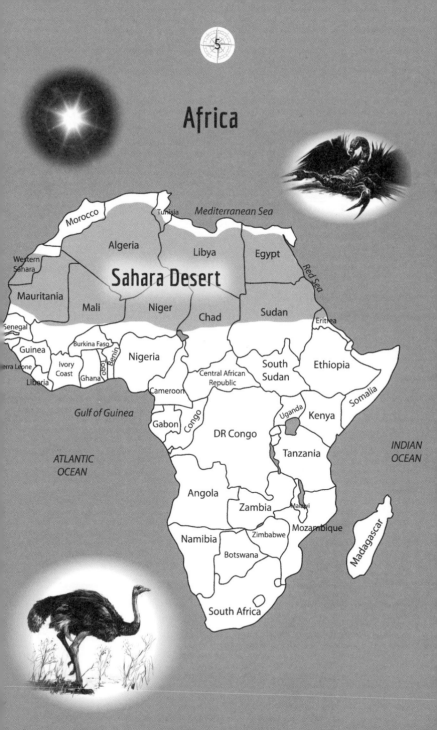

Mediterranean Sea

Morocco

Tunisia

Algeria

Libya

Egypt

Western Sahara

Sahara Desert

Red Sea

Mauritania

Mali

Niger

Chad

Sudan

Eritrea

Senegal

Guinea

Burkina Faso

Nigeria

Sierra Leone

Ivory Coast

Ghana

Togo

Benin

Central African Republic

South Sudan

Ethiopia

Liberia

Cameroon

Somalia

Gulf of Guinea

Gabon

Congo

DR Congo

Uganda

Kenya

ATLANTIC OCEAN

Tanzania

INDIAN OCEAN

Angola

Zambia

Malawi

Mozambique

Madagascar

Namibia

Zimbabwe

Botswana

South Africa

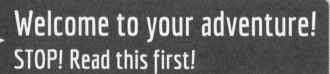

Welcome to your adventure!
STOP! Read this first!

Welcome to an action-packed adventure in which you take the starring role!

You're about to enter the Sahara Desert, one of the most inhospitable places on Earth. On each page, choose from different options—according to your instincts, knowledge, and intelligence—and make your own path through the desert to safety.

You decide:
- How to escape a deadly scorpion;
- Where to find water in a parched desert landscape;
- How to handle a pack of hungry hyenas;

…and many more life-or-death dilemmas. Along the way, you'll discover the facts you need to help you survive.

It's time to test your survival skills—or die trying!

Your adventure starts on page 7.

You open your eyes and blink quickly to get rid of the sand. You're lying on the desert floor with your backpack next to you, completely covered by a blanket.

It's swelteringly hot. You throw the blanket off and, with it, a thick layer of fine sand that also seems to have found its way into your hair, nose, eyes, and clothes. The sun is so dazzling that you have to shield your eyes. You look around you. The arid desert landscape stretches as far as you can see in every direction.

You piece together the events that led you here: you were on a camel safari, part of a group of 10 people, including two knowledgeable guides. A sandstorm blew up. The noise of the howling wind and the sand flying in all directions was confusing and disorienting. You thought you were following everyone else, but you must have been stumbling blindly in the wrong direction. There's a movement in the bright blue sky. A dark shape circles overhead. You gulp: it's a vulture.

There is no one to be seen. The sun beats down relentlessly. You are completely lost and, as far as you can tell, totally alone. You know you need to find help. But where?

You set off with nothing but the clothes on your back and your backpack, which contains a few useful things that might help you in your journey.

How will you survive?

Turn to page 8 to find information you need to help you survive.

The Sahara Desert is the largest hot desert in the world. It stretches for more than 3.5 million square miles (9.1 million sq km) across most of the northern part of Africa, from the Atlantic Ocean in the west to the Red Sea in the east. It covers large parts of Algeria, Chad, Egypt, Libya, Mali, Mauritania, Morocco, Niger, Western Sahara, Sudan, and Tunisia. The Sahara is one of the hottest places on Earth and one of the most hostile. People have walked into the vast, scorching desert never to return. If you're going to survive, you'll need to have your wits about you.

Desert Perils

The desert's lack of water is the greatest peril for any traveler (find out more on pages 49 and 81). Danger also lurks in the form of deadly scorpions and snakes. The deathstalker scorpion is one of the most deadly on Earth; the saw-scaled viper is responsible for thousands of human deaths every year. There are also larger animals that might prove to be a threat: baboons, ostriches, hyenas, and jackals.

Saharan Landscape

Think of the Sahara and you probably imagine enormous dunes of fine, shifting sand. Sand dunes like this, known as ergs, take up about 20% of the Sahara Desert and can rise up to 590 feet (180 m) high. Most of the desert is made up of dry, rocky plains, called regs. Hamadas are large areas of exposed rock, which have been worn smooth by the wind. There are mountains in the Sahara, too. The highest peak reaches more than 11,150 feet (3,400 m) high. Other than the Nile River, there are no permanent rivers or streams in the Sahara. Seasonal rivers and streams are known as wadis. Most of the time, they're dry. Water reaches the surface at oases.

Desert Life

It might look like a lifeless wasteland, but some plants and animals thrive in the hot, dry conditions of the Sahara. Plants include the baobab and acacia trees, as well as grasses and shrubs. Some plants, such as date palms, that grow near wadis or oases have long roots that reach underground water reserves. Animals include jerboas (small rodents), addax (a type of antelope), Barbary sheep, and camels (introduced to the Sahara around 200 CE). Other desert animals include deadly scorpions, spiders, ants, and venomous snakes. Most people who live in the Sahara live near the oases. There are also nomads, who are people that herd animals and trade goods between oases and cities on the edges of the desert.

Dry Desert

Deserts are defined by their lack of precipitation. They receive less than ten inches (250 mm) of rain per year. In the Sahara, most regions receive less than five inches (130 mm) of rain on average, though it rains more in the mountains. Rainfall is highly variable—some areas might have no rain at all for a number of years, then 20 inches (500 mm) might fall in a sudden downpour.

Sizzling Sun

During the day, the Sahara is hot. Temperatures of around 100 degrees Fahrenheit (38 degrees Celsius) are common, but it can reach more than 122°F (50°C). The highest temperature ever recorded in the Sahara was a blistering 136°F (58°C)! At night, the temperature plummets. It can go down to 32°F (0°C) in parts of the desert. During the winter months, the temperature often falls below freezing at night.

Turn to page 10.

Desert Survival Tips

Here are a few basic tips that might affect your chances of survival in the desert:

- Water is your first priority, and you need to be aware of how much you need. This varies dramatically according to temperature and whether you are using energy. You might be surprised at how much water you need in hot conditions. Someone working strenuously in the heat of 100°F (38°C) would need five gallons (20 L) of water a day! However, it can also be very dangerous to consume too much water. A chart on page 119 helps explain water consumption.

- Keep your skin covered—it will burn very easily if you don't. Loose clothing will help keep you cooler as you sweat. The wet cloth against your skin will cool you down. Cover your head, too—if you don't, you risk getting heatstroke.

- You need salt, too, because you lose salt as you sweat.

- Don't eat—it will only make you thirstier.

- Breathe through your nose to conserve as much moisture as possible.

- The temperature drops dramatically at night, so make sure you have something warm to wrap up in.

- If you have no idea at all where you are, you are probably better off staying in one place, signaling if you can, and waiting to be rescued. But where's the fun in that?

Even though the sun isn't at its highest point in the sky, it is still blisteringly hot. You dread to think what the temperature will be like at midday, as you stagger across the barren, rocky ground toward the meager shade offered by a large boulder. You sit down while you decide what to do.

You could stay put and wait to be rescued—maybe you could spell out SOS with rocks. On the other hand, you could easily die of thirst before help arrives. You think about it for awhile. Finally, you decide you must do something. Just sitting around waiting will drive you crazy!

You check inside your backpack. Things could be a lot worse. You were one of the water carriers in your group, so you have one gallon (4 L) of water in plastic bottles. You take a grateful swig from one of them. There are also matches in your backpack, which will come in handy for making fires, as well as several other useful items including a spade, sunblock, and a small aluminum pot, which you can use to boil water. You're dressed properly for the desert in a loose cotton shirt, pants, and a scarf that you can wrap around your face in case of another sandstorm. You also have a blanket for the cold night.

The water you have probably won't last very long if you walk in this terrible heat, so you'll have to find another water source pretty quickly. Your water will last much longer if you rest during the day and travel at night, though.

If you decide to go in search of water, turn to page 26.

If you decide to rest now, shelter from the sun, and travel later, turn to page 22.

You feel as though you're being slowly roasted. The trees seem much farther away than you thought. It can be hard to judge distances in the desert, because there aren't any of the objects you'd normally use for reference—cars, lampposts, people. A pile of rocks could be small and quite close, or large and far away. The same goes for trees, especially if you're not familiar with the type. You're sweating so much that your cotton shirt is drenched, and your backpack feels heavier than ever. Maybe if you took off some of your clothes you might feel a bit cooler.

If you decide to take off some clothes, go to page 16.

If you decide to carry on as you are, go to page 35.

You wriggle out of the cave. You're right to be careful of dark, enclosed spaces—there could be snakes or other creatures lurking in there. And, in fact, there were deadly scorpions in that cave!

You make yourself comfortable in the shade. Even though you're still hot, resting and keeping as cool as you can is the best policy in the desert during the day. At night, the temperature drops dramatically. You'll be able to move around then, and the exercise will keep you warm. You rest and doze, making sure you take sips of water whenever you're awake.

As dusk begins to fall, you spot a dry stream bed with a pile of stones in it. You decide to go investigate in search of water.

Go to page 28.

You approach the feeding pack. Most of the jackals scatter, but three remain, feeding on the animal carcass of what looks like a young gazelle. The meat looks fresh and isn't smelly, so it must be a recent kill. The jackals seem to be nervous animals, so you're not worried. You think about using some of your matches to get a fire going to roast some of the meat.

You're a short distance from the dead animal. Two of the jackals lope off, but the remaining one growls at you and bares its teeth. You wave your arms, expecting it to run away, but it runs toward you. You aim a kick, but miss. The jackal bites your arm. You cry out in pain. The wound isn't bleeding much, but it's very painful. You aim another kick at the jackal, and it runs off to join the rest of its pack.

You sit down, feeling faint. You know that all members of the dog family are host to a wide variety of bacteria in their mouths, so you use some of your water to wash the wound. The bleeding soon stops. Unfortunately, despite the fact that you poured water on the wound, the jackal has given you blood poisoning, also known as sepsis. Soon the wound is red, painful, and oozing pus. You feel weak and dizzy, and have to lie down. Alone and without medical attention, you're too weak to find more water. The infection and lack of water soon kill you.

The end.

Jackals

- There are three species of African jackals: the common or golden jackal, the side-striped jackal, and the black-backed jackal. The golden jackal lives in northern Africa. It's also the biggest, at about three feet (1 m) long and one and a half feet (0.5 m) up to its shoulder.

- Jackals usually hunt alone or in pairs, although bigger family groups sometimes hunt in packs. Groups might gather to feed on carrion.

- Jackals eat a wide variety of food. They prey on rodents, small mammals, lizards, snakes, carrion, fruit, insects (including dungbeetles), and even young gazelles. They attack animals up to three times their own weight. However, it's extremely unusual for them to attack a human being—they will usually run away.

- Jackals are crepuscular, or active at dawn and dusk, to avoid the heat of the desert sun.

You take off your shirt and pants, but you don't feel any better, and soon you put your clothes back on, realizing that you were cooler before anyway. The skin across your shoulders stings as you put your shirt back on.

By the time you get to the parched-looking trees, you're sunburned, exhausted, and dehydrated. There's no visible water. Wearily, you begin to dig—but this just makes you sweat even more. You soon develop heat exhaustion, then heatstroke. You crawl into a patch of shade under a tree. Your last thought is that you should have rested until nightfall.

The end.

→ Heatstroke

- Heat exhaustion occurs when the body temperature rises above 98°F (37°C), which can be treated by drinking water and keeping cool.

- Heatstroke occurs when the body temperature is above 104°F (40°C). Victims can become confused and have shallow, quick breathing.

- If heatstroke isn't treated immediately, the body overheats and organs stop functioning normally, eventually leading to death.

You're pretty sure this is south. Ahead of you stretches a gravelly, arid plain, with dunes in the distance. It doesn't look very promising. But you trudge off, using the dunes and a rocky escarpment to your right to keep you on your course.

Go to page 50.

Unknown to you, there are scorpions in this shallow cave, sheltering from the heat of the day just as you are. One, a large deathstalker, is scuttling farther back into the cave to get away from you when you move your foot and kick it by accident. Alarmed, the scorpion raises its deadly sting and strikes, injecting a lethal dose of venom into your ankle.

The pain from the sting is agonizing. You curse yourself for not checking inside first as you hurriedly move out of the cave to avoid risking another sting. You don't know what's stung you, but you remember there are dangerous scorpions in the Sahara.

Your ankle becomes numb. You use some water to wash it, in case that helps. Unfortunately, it doesn't. Your tongue becomes swollen, you feel dizzy and feverish, and your heart races. You begin to have difficulty swallowing and breathing.

It's not long before the scorpion's venom kills you.

The end.

Deathstalker Scorpions

- The deathstalker scorpion is one of the world's most venomous scorpions. Despite this, a sting from a deathstalker wouldn't usually kill a healthy adult human—though the sting is extremely painful. If you are sick, or if you're a child or an older person, you're in more danger.

- Deathstalkers are found in North Africa and the Middle East. They can grow up to about four inches (10 cm) long and are yellowish in color.

- They prey on insects and spiders. Their pincers are weak, which is why their venom is so powerful—so that it kills prey quickly to stop it from escaping the scorpion's grasp.

- Along with most other scorpions, deathstalkers are nocturnal, spending the day in burrows or under rocks.

- There are more than 1,500 different species of scorpions. Most live in desert regions, but there are also scorpions that live in rain forests and temperate regions.

- In times of food shortage, scorpions are able to lower their metabolic rate so they can survive long periods—up to a year—without eating.

- Scorpions usually prey on insects and other invertebrates, but they'll eat almost anything, including other scorpions.

Movement catches your eye: in the twilight, you spot a snake side-winding down a sand dune, leaving a regular pattern behind it. It's a sand viper that preys mostly on lizards. You watch as it moves gracefully off on its nighttime hunt.

The dunes stretch into the distance, where they look as though they must be several stories high.

Should you trek along the sand dune or find another route? Another route will mean changing from your chosen course.

If you decide to alter your course away from the sand dune, turn to page 50.

If you decide to walk along the dune, turn to page 44.

The building is little more than a tiny mud hut, half falling down, but it provides all the shade you need. After checking for creatures, you spread out your blanket and rest all day out of the intense heat, making sure you drink enough water. As dusk descends and the temperature rapidly cools, you pick up your things and decide which direction to take.

But your attention is caught by some noises outside the building. You investigate and discover a group of what look like dogs in the distance. You recognize them as jackals. It looks as though they've found a dead animal to eat.

As long as the animal is recently dead, you could chase away the jackals, then make a fire and cook some of the meat for yourself.

If you decide to shoo away the jackals from their food, go to page 14.

If you decide to steer clear of the animals, go to page 36.

You scan the landscape for somewhere suitable to shelter from the sun for the day. There's a ridge of higher ground with plenty of big boulders that should provide shade. Or, farther away, you can see what looks like a small rectangular building.

If you decide to head for the building, go to page 21.

If you decide to shelter among the rocks, go to page 51.

Shelter in the Desert

- When you're sheltering in the daytime in the desert, your first priority is shade. You can find natural shade in rocky areas, and you might even find deserted buildings. You could also use a bush for shelter with a blanket or other covering thrown over it.

- Shelters below ground can reduce the desert heat considerably, but first consider the amount of effort needed to dig and whether it's worth it. If it's already hot, don't bother digging a shelter as you'll use up too much water by sweating.

- If it's not too hot yet, you could try digging a trench about 20 inches (50 cm) deep, and long and wide enough for you to lie down in comfortably. Pile earth or sand from your trench around three sides, leaving the fourth side open for you to enter and exit the shelter. Secure your blanket or other covering over the top. Ideally, the outer covering should be white to reflect the heat, and you should have a second layer underneath it, with an air pocket in between.

- If you're sheltering at night in the desert, you need to keep as warm as possible. Make sure there's something underneath you and don't lie on the cold ground. Don't make your shelter in a valley bottom, which will be especially cold and prone to frost.

- Wherever you're sheltering in the desert, make sure it's free from insects and reptiles that might give you a nasty bite or sting.

- Always avoid areas that could flood in a sudden downpour, such as dry river beds. However unlikely it seems, flash floods do happen in deserts.

Deciding to carry on even though the temperature is above 85°F (30°C), was not a good idea. The sun is now burning any exposed skin on your body. Even though you've been drinking lots of water, your body has been sweating heavily, losing salt as a result.

The very low salt levels in your body have led to hyponatremia. Your body is unable to process water, making the cells in your body expand. As the cells in your brain expand, you feel dizzy and confused. It's not long before you're forced to lie down. You fall into a coma and die.

The end.

Hyponatremia

- We need salt to live. Hyponatremia is a low level of salt in the blood.

- It can be caused by drinking too much water (yes, even water can be bad for you). For example, hyponatremia can occur if you drink a lot of water but don't replace the salt that you've lost after sweating during a workout at the gym or if you've lost a lot of body fluids due to severe diarrhea or vomiting. Hyponatremia can also be caused by kidney failure and heart failure, as well as some other conditions.

- When salt is low, the body's cells swell up with water. When brain cells swell, it's especially dangerous because the skull limits how much the brain can expand, causing it to press on the skull.

- Symptoms of hyponatremia include headache, confusion, tiredness, nausea, muscle spasms, and seizures.

- In severe cases, hyponatremia can be fatal.

You gaze across the barren landscape. A smudge of green catches your eye. In the distance, you can make out a clump of trees—that must mean water!

You put on sunglasses, make a head covering out of a spare white shirt in your backpack, and set off. The bottles of water in your backpack are heavy, and almost right away your back is soaked with sweat.

Crossing the gravelly, dry plain toward the trees, you are baking hot, but you're convinced that finding water should be your top priority in the desert.

Go to page 12.

Adapting for the Desert

As a human, you're not particularly well equipped for desert survival. Desert plants and animals have adapted to cope with the hot, dry conditions.

- Most desert animals are nocturnal, taking advantage of the cool of the night. They spend the hot days resting, many of them in cool underground burrows.

- Some animals don't need to drink water at all—they get the moisture they need from the plants or animals they eat. The addax, for example, is a large Saharan antelope that gets water from sucking on plants.

- Many desert animals conserve water by not sweating, and passing only small amounts of urine.

- Some animals cool down by peeing on their legs! Turkey vultures do this.

- Because fat increases body heat, some animals have adapted by concentrating their body fat in one place, such as in a hump on a camel or at the base of the tail in some lizards.

- Some desert plants store water in their roots, stems, leaves, or fruit. The baobab tree, for example, stores water in its trunk. It gets fatter and thinner at different times of year, depending on how much water it's storing.

- Desert plants' leaves might be glossy, to reflect the sun, and/or waxy to keep moisture in.

- Some desert plants have very long roots that reach down to underground water supplies. Others have shallow roots that take advantage of surface water.

As you reach the pile of stones in the gloomy dusk light, you're even more convinced that they have been placed there deliberately. You move them and, sure enough, they're covering a water hole.

You take some water in your cupped hands—it looks and smells clean. Should you bother to make a fire to boil it? It would be time-consuming, and you can't imagine what could possibly contaminate it.

If you decide to make a fire to boil the water, go to page 45.

If you decide not to bother boiling the water, and go ahead and fill up your containers, go to page 46.

Making a Fire in the Desert

- Dry desert conditions are perfect for making a fire. The main problem, especially here in the Sahara, is fuel. You need tinder (flammable material such as wood shavings), kindling (small twigs), and fuel (larger pieces of wood for when the fire is burning well). Gather any wood you see in the Sahara. If you can't find any wood, you could try dried animal droppings!

- Choose a sheltered spot for your fire where the wind won't blow it out, and make sure it's not too near a tree or other plants that could catch fire. If the wind is very strong, you might need to dig a trench to make your fire. Put a circle of rocks around it to conserve the heat and fuel.

- Make a bed of tinder (this could be dry grass) and make a tepee of kindling around it. Light the tinder with a match. Only start adding larger pieces of wood when the kindling is burning well.

- Luckily you have some matches with you but, if you didn't, you would have to try to create a spark using friction to light your tinder. This could simply be rubbing two sticks together, but a fire plow is a more sophisticated method: cut a groove in a flat piece of wood, then rub a sharpened stick up and down it. The stick will need to be harder wood than the flat piece. This will create shavings that act as tinder, which will catch fire from a spark.

- During the day, you could ignite kindling by directing the sun's rays through a lens or the bottom of a glass bottle.

You sit down in a small patch of shade and scan the landscape for somewhere to rest. You take a drink and rummage at the bottom of your backpack for a packet of salt, which you sprinkle into the bottle— you've been sweating so much that you probably need a salt boost.

In the distance, you spot what looks like a small rectangular building. It might be a good place to rest for the day. As the sun beats down, you can see that it was foolish to try to walk in the desert during the day when it's burning hot. It's much better to rest now, then set off in search of rescue when the temperature drops at dusk.

Go to page 21.

It's dark inside the small cave. It's soothing to your eyes, which ache from the brightness of the sun. It's cooler, too. You've got a much better chance of resting comfortably here. You move a few small rocks and pebbles and put the blanket underneath you to make a soft bed.

Suddenly you hear scuttling in the cave. There are probably other animals in here that are sheltering from the heat, too. Should you move from your comfortable position?

If you decide to move, go to page 13.

If you decide to stay where you are, go to page 18.

The snake is a saw-scaled viper, one of the most venomous and aggressive snakes in Africa. This one was out hunting when you got too close. It loops its body into S shapes, rubbing its scales together. This makes a warning noise like a hiss. Because you haven't backed off, it strikes lightning fast.

The snake has bitten your ankle. You stagger backward, away from the snake, in agonizing pain. The bite starts to swell. Soon you feel feverish and begin to vomit. You need anti-venom and hospital care but, alone in the middle of the desert, you're not going to get it. The snake's venom stops blood from clotting and leads to kidney failure.

The end.

Saw-scaled Vipers

- There are eight species of saw-scaled vipers that live north of the equator across Africa, Arabia, and southwestern Asia, including India and Sri Lanka.

- They're between about 12 inches (30 cm) and three and a half feet (1 m) long, with a thick body. They can be brown, gray, or orange, with darker spots and blotches. They have serrated scales, which make the hissing noise you heard when they are rubbed together. They use it as a warning, like a rattlesnake's rattle.

- The snakes are nocturnal, feeding on small mammals, birds, lizards, scorpions, and other invertebrates.

- Saw-scaled vipers are extremely aggressive, and their venom is very powerful.

- There are snakes with more powerful venom. But, where saw-scaled vipers are found, they're responsible for more human deaths than all other snakes in the region put together.

- The snakes cause thousands of deaths per year. They live in unpopulated areas of the Sahara, as well as in close proximity to people.

You set off again. It's chilly, and you're glad of the blanket around your shoulders.

You spot a movement from the corner of your eye. There are some rocks just beside you, and you thought you saw something climbing them. You investigate—and come face to face with a gorgeous, fluffy cat. It has big ears and a very cute face and it's looking at you in surprise.

You're not sure if it's some kind of wild desert cat or a domestic cat. If it's a house cat, there must be people nearby. Should you pat it, and let it lead you to where it lives?

If you decide to approach the cat, go to page 58.

If you decide to leave it alone, go to page 54.

You've never felt so hot. Sweat drenches your clothes and trickles down the sides of your face as you walk. Something glints in the sunlight. To your horror, you see it's the bleached bones of a large dead animal, its ribs pointing toward the sky.

A shiver runs down your spine despite the extreme heat. You're feeling a bit dizzy, too—maybe it's the sight of the animal skeleton.

Perhaps it's time to admit defeat and find shelter from the sun, then walk at night instead.

If you decide to seek shelter, go to page 30.

If you decide to keep going, go to page 24.

The sun is beginning to slip below the horizon. You know that the sun sets in the west, so now it will be easier for you to figure out which way is north, south, east, and west. You are sure you don't want to go north because you set off for your desert trek at the southern edge of the desert. You reckon the direction you should take to go away from the desert is south or southwest of where you are now.

You point the number 12 on your watch face in the direction of the sun. So, which way should you go?

If you decide to follow the direction of the number 6, go to page 20.

If you decide to follow the number 9, go to page 17.

If you decide to follow the number 10, go to page 48.

Using a Watch as a Compass

If the sun isn't conveniently setting or rising, another way you can figure out which way is north, south, east, and west is by using a watch with hands.

- With the watch in the palm of your hand, point the hour hand toward the sun (but don't look at the sun or you could damage your eyes).

- In the northern hemisphere, the sun is due south at midday. That means you can work out which way is south by dividing the angle between the hour hand (which is the position of the sun now) and the 12 on the watch face in half. So, at 2 o'clock in the afternoon, the number 1 would be halfway between the 12 and the 2 on the watch face, pointing toward the south.

- If you only have a digital watch, just draw a clock face in the sand with the hour hand pointing at the sun.

- If you don't know what the time is, stand a stick in the sand and measure its shadow at different times of day. In the northern hemisphere, the shortest shadow will point north.

- At night, you can find north if you know which star is Polaris, the North Star.

After jogging and walking awhile, you feel a bit winded. You pause, looking back to where you first started out. The rock, next to its withered tree, seems a long way away now. You've covered a lot of ground.

Even though the night is cold, you're very warm from the effort. You are tired and sweating from carrying your heavy backpack. Maybe you should slow down.

If you decide to slow down, go to page 74.

If you carry on jogging and walking, go to page 80.

It's dusk, and the temperature is already dropping dramatically. The sun is slipping over the horizon quickly—twilight doesn't last for long when you're this close to the equator. You get up and shake out your blanket. Soon it will be cold enough to wrap it around you as you walk.

Not very far away from you, there's a wadi—a dry river bed. There's a pile of stones in it, which look as though they might have been deliberately placed on top of one another. Should you go and investigate, or is it better to figure out which direction you need to head in before you do anything else?

If you decide to figure out your direction first, go to page 36.

If you decide to investigate the stones in the wadi, go to page 28.

As you get closer to the high ground, you realize there are more hyenas than you thought—they seem to be everywhere. They're bigger than you thought, too. Still, you reason, hyenas are cowardly scavengers. And anyway, who could be frightened of an animal that laughs?

You should be frightened, though, because hyenas are dangerous animals that have been known to attack and kill people. A few of them lope toward you, spreading out to your right and left. You're worried now—but it's too late. Two of the hyenas run at you and attack. At least it's all over pretty quickly.

The end.

Spotted Hyenas

- There are four types of hyenas—brown, striped, aardwolf, and spotted. Spotted hyenas are the largest species. They are huge, measuring up to about five feet (1.5 m) long, and weigh as much as 175 pounds (80 kg)! They live mainly in sub-Saharan Africa.

- They don't just scavenge food. Hyenas are also skilled pack hunters that prey on animals as large as wildebeest.

- Spotted hyenas make a variety of noises to communicate with one another, including their famous "laugh."

- They live together in large groups of up to about 100 animals. Female hyenas, which are larger than males, lead the group.

- Despite their appearance, hyenas are more closely related to cats than dogs.

- Hyenas' jaws are extremely powerful—capable of crunching bones. They can even digest teeth, so nothing goes to waste.

- Hyenas will attack and kill people, sometimes even dragging people from their beds at night.

You shelter at the base of the dune as the wind howls even louder, and sand and grit whirl through the air in choking clouds. Soon it's impossible to see anything in the swirling sandstorm. You cover up any exposed areas of your body because the sandy wind feels like sandpaper on your bare skin.

Unfortunately, you've picked the wrong place to shelter. Unless there's thunder and lightning, when you could run the risk of a lightning strike, it's better to head for higher ground in a sandstorm, because the sand, grit, and dust are denser the lower down you are. And a dune was an especially bad place to pick—since it is made entirely of sand! The wind picks up truckloads of sand, dumping it back down on you, burying you completely underneath a thick, suffocating layer.

The end.

Sandstorms

- Sandstorms are caused by strong winds blowing over loose sand or earth. Most are small and last only a matter of minutes. The biggest can be more than half a mile (1 km) high, more than 100 miles (160 km) wide, and can travel at 75 miles (120 km) per hour.

- It's very easy to become lost in a sandstorm. That's how you ended up lost in the desert in the first place. The whirling sand makes it impossible to see. It's best not to move around, since it's easy to become disoriented.

- The best thing to do is find shelter (though not by a sand dune), cover your nose and mouth with cloth, and wrap the rest of your body in whatever you have on hand to stop the sand and grit from hurting your skin. Then wait the sandstorm out.

Walking on the sand dune is a bit like walking through deep snow—your feet sink deep into the sand, and every step takes a huge effort. Despite the cold, you're starting to sweat. The dune is enormous, and stretches far off into the distance in the bright moonlight. Maybe you should find easier terrain.

If you decide to turn back, altering your course, go to page 50.

If you decide to carry on walking on the dune, go to page 64.

You're almost optimistic about your situation now that you've got plenty of water. You're feeling pretty fit, the moon is bright enough to see by, and you're not too cold as long as you keep moving.

The desert looks endless—mile after mile of scrubby, almost featureless rocky landscape. The desert is so big, it could take a long time to find help. You remember hearing that the most efficient way to cover ground is to jog for a few paces, then walk for a few paces. This is how soldiers cover ground quickly. Maybe you should do the same.

If you decide to jog and walk, go to page 38.

If you decide to just walk, go to page 74.

Did you really think it was a good idea not to bother boiling the water? Oh dear.

You don't realize it for a few days, but you've contracted amoebic dysentery from the water, which gives you bad diarrhea, vomiting, pain, and fever. The diarrhea on its own is enough to kill you, since you're unable to replace the lost fluids and salts. You need medical care to recover… and…well…

The end.

Dysentery

- There are two types of dysentery, one caused by bacteria and the other caused by amoebas, or single-celled parasites that live in your intestines.

- Both types of dysentery can be passed on through poor hygiene or by consuming contaminated food or water. In some people, amoebic dysentery can be life-threatening.

- Symptoms of amoebic dysentery include diarrhea, stomach pain, vomiting, and fever.

- Amoebic dysentery is treated with medicine. If can be fatal.

The bite is so painful it feels as though it's throbbing, and the scratches are sore, too. You decide to take a chance by using some of your valuable water. First you take a long swig, then you use some of the water to wash the wounds. The small holes where the cat's teeth punctured your skin are very painful to the touch, but you reason that washing them can't possibly do any harm. You know you don't have any soap, but you rummage around in your backpack for something that might help. To your surprise and relief, you discover a tube of antiseptic cream. You apply the cream, and wrap a spare cotton scarf around the bite and the scratches. Before long, you're feeling much better.

Now you need to find more water to replenish the water you used to wash your wounds.

Go to page 64.

You set off on your course, just to the left of the setting sun. The temperature is dropping fast. Before long, you spot something that looks like a building and hurry toward it.

As you get closer, you can see that the small adobe building has long since been abandoned—half of it is in ruins. You investigate and discover a low, circular wall with a heavy wooden cover on it. You can hardly believe your eyes—could this actually be a well? You take off the cover and peer inside. The reflection of the bright moon glints at the bottom! There's a rope with a plastic bucket to drop down. It plops into the water with a satisfying splash and you bring up some water. The bucket leaks a bit, but it works. You drink some water and fill up your bottles.

It occurs to you that you could stay here and wait to be rescued. On the other hand, it doesn't look like anyone has been here for a very long time.

If you decide to stay here and await rescue, go to page 63.

If you decide to move on with your full water bottles, go to page 34.

Desert Wells and Water Holes

- If you find a well or water hole in the desert, make sure you replace the cover quickly to prevent evaporation or contamination of the water.

- You might find an animal water hole in the desert, but be careful—the water could be contaminated with animal feces and other bacteria. One option is to dig another hole close to the water hole so that, as the new hole fills with water, it is filtered through the sand and gravel. This removes some of the impurities. Then boil the water.

- The nomadic people of the Sahara know exactly where the water holes are so that they can replenish their water supplies as they move through the desert. They have to be precise—just a few miles in the wrong direction could end in disaster.

- If you spot flies, mosquitoes, or bees, it's a sign that water isn't far away.

- Birds can point the way to desert water sources. Watch the direction of their flight in the evenings.

Suddenly you hear a sound that sends a shiver down your spine—a rasping, hissing sound. You stop dead in your tracks. You look down to where you think the noise is coming from. At first you can't see anything on the sandy, pebbly ground. Then you spot it! A snake is curving its body into S-shaped loops. The loops are making the rasping sound as they slide against one another. You're almost standing on it!

It's just a small snake. It's probably more frightened of you than you are of it, right? And you know that most snakes aren't venomous. Should you just ignore it? Or should you back away and run?

If you decide to step around the snake, go to page 32.

If you decide to run away, go to page 62.

The rocks offer shade from the fierce sun. They're tall, and there are enough of them to allow you to rest in the shade without having to move when the sun shifts across the sky. Although you're still baking hot, you no longer feel as though you're being roasted over a spit. You spread your blanket out on the ground and lie down, feeling better by the minute.

You're just about to close your eyes when you notice that there's a small, dark cave in the rocks. The entrance is big enough for you to crawl into, but not much bigger than that. It would be even cooler in there, where the sun hasn't warmed up the sand.

If you decide to crawl into the cave, go to page 31.

If you decide to rest where you are in the shade of the rocks, go to page 39.

Off to your right, you spot movement. It's a small herd of antelope, heading away from you. Maybe they've been drinking at a water hole?

You follow them and find that they've finished their drink. The moonlight glints on a small pool of water that the antelope must have just visited. Because the water hole is used by animals, you decide to be on the safe side: you dig a hole a short distance from the pool and wait for water to seep into it. That way, it's filtered by the sand. While you're waiting, you make a fire (see page 29) and boil the water. It takes a while, but you eventually fill up all your bottles. At least you can be fairly sure the water isn't going to make you sick.

Go to page 84.

Cats have bacteria-ridden mouths, and a very nasty infection has started in your wrist where the sand cat bit you. The wound is inflamed, painful, and oozing with pus. You pour some of your water on it but, by this time, the infection has taken hold.

The wrist is an especially bad place to be bitten because it's full of blood vessels and tendons, so an infection can be spread around the body to vital organs very quickly. You start to feel weak and sick, and you realize you won't be able to continue walking. Eventually, you stop by some rocks. You can see that there should be shade here in the daytime. There's no water source nearby, but the infection kills you before you run out anyway.

The end.

On the ground in front of you, there's a vine-like plant bearing fruit that look like small melons—roughly about the size of oranges. Melons are famous for being juicy. They would help keep you hydrated and give you some energy for walking at the same time. On the other hand, although the fruit look like melons, you're not absolutely sure what they are. They could even be poisonous!

If you decide to eat the fruit, go to page 68.

If you decide not to, go to page 50.

Edible Desert Plants

- The African baobab tree stores drinkable water in its trunk, and the pulp in its fruit is tasty and nutritious. The trees can be over 80 feet (25 m) tall and can live for 3,000 years. They're known as upside-down trees because the branches look like roots.

- The fruit of the wild desert gourd (see page 69) can't be eaten, but the seeds can and the shoots can be chewed to obtain water.

- The Topnaar tribe of the Namib Desert depend on the !nara plant. Its tasty fruit is harvested once a year, and its seeds are dried and eaten as a delicacy.

- In the deserts of North America, cacti can be sources of food and water. The pulp of the fishhook barrel cactus can be squeezed to obtain water (although the water can taste horrible!), and its fruits and flesh are edible.

- The agave (also from North America) collects rainwater at the base of the plant, and some moisture is stored in its leaves and stalk.

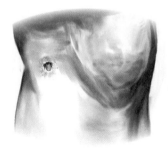

You should have removed the tick because, unfortunately, it has passed on bacteria via its bite. You don't get any symptoms for a while, but then you start to feel feverish. Soon you have a terrible headache, as well as muscle and joint pain all over your body.

You have relapsing fever, which needs to be treated with antibiotics. The disease wouldn't normally kill a healthy person, but it makes you feel so ill that you aren't capable of finding water.

The end.

Parasite-borne Diseases

- Relapsing fever can be caused by ticks or lice, and both types are common in Africa. Symptoms wouldn't usually appear for at least five days. It's worse if the disease is passed on by lice, and you might die if you don't take antibiotics. Even if victims are treated, one in a hundred will die anyway. Epidemics of louse-borne relapsing fever sometimes happen where living conditions are poor.

- Malaria is caused by the plasmodium parasite, which gets into the blood through the bite of a female anopheles mosquito. Symptoms usually appear around 10 days after the bite, but sometimes they can take up to a year to appear. Over a million people, mostly in Africa, die from malaria every year because they aren't treated in time.

- Tsetse fly bites can pass on a disease known as sleeping sickness, caused by a parasite that infects the flies. There are two types of sleeping sickness. If you get the severe form, you will almost certainly die without treatment.

You approach the cat with your hand outstretched. Its eyes widen. Suddenly it flattens its large ears to its head and hisses at you, baring its pointed teeth. You remove your hand quickly, and you're just about to run away when the cat launches itself at you and sinks its teeth into your wrist, scratching your arms with its claws at the same time.

You manage to fling it off. The cat bounds away into the night.

If you decide to return to the well and the ruins for water to wash your wounds, go to page 73.

If you decide to wrap a bandage around the wound and keep going, go to page 61.

Sand Cats

- Sand cats are the only type of cat that live in deserts. They're found in both stony and sandy deserts in northern Africa, and southwest and central Asia.

- They are sandy colored, sometimes with stripes on their fur, with a ringed tail with a dark tip. They can measure up to two feet (60 cm) long, including the tail.

- These cats are able to survive without water, getting the moisture they need from their food, though they will drink if they find water.

- Sand cats eat small mammals, such as jerboas, gerbils, lizards, and insects. They sometimes dig out their prey from under the ground.

- They live in burrows, where they stay during the day in the hottest months, only coming out to hunt at dusk and during the night.

You make it safely past the hyenas. But as you walk on, you become aware of an uncomfortable spot on your leg. Eventually you decide to stop and take a look at it. To your horror, you see that it's alive!

The creature is a tick, a small parasite that feeds on the blood of mammals. This one has decided to have a snack at your expense.

You have no idea whether ticks can do any harm—after all, they're very small—but you do know that leeches will attach themselves to people and drink their blood without doing any harm at all. Maybe, like leeches, the tick will just drop off when it's had enough. Or maybe you should try to remove it.

If you decide to ignore the tick, go to page 56.

If you decide to remove it, go to page 89.

The pain in your arm makes you stop to examine your wounds. The scratches aren't deep, but the bite on your wrist looks red and angry, and your hand is beginning to swell.

Should you just keep going, or is it better to find water, wash the wound, and have a rest?

If you decide to keep going, go to page 53.

If you decide to stop and treat the wound, go to page 47.

Thankfully, you make it safely away from the snake. You round the summit of a low hill and a wonderful sight is waiting for you on the other side—a few palm trees, clustered together. It must mean a spring or a well!

You spot a well among the trees. You're heading straight for it when something alarming happens: you sink straight down into the ground!

Quicksand! Thinking fast, you throw your blanket over onto solid ground. It's cold in the quicksand, and you'll need it when you get out . . . if you get out. The quicksand is up to your waist now. Should you risk trying to throw your heavy backpack to the safety of solid ground? You could lose everything if it falls in.

If you decide to keep your backpack on, go to page 78.

If you decide to throw it to the side, go to page 86.

There's plenty of water for you to drink in the well, though there's nothing for you to eat. Luckily, you have enough packets of salt in your backpack to ensure that you don't get hyponatremia (see page 25).

You exist for weeks, sheltering from the sun during the day and exercising at night to keep warm, making sure you don't stray too far and get lost. You've started talking to yourself. At first you're tempted to try to kill a lizard or a jerboa to eat, but they're too fast for you. After a while you stop feeling hungry anyway, and you start talking to the lizards instead. They don't reply.

After several weeks alone in the desert, you start to feel very weak from lack of food. One day, you spot a camel train heading for the well. You can hardly believe it—in fact, you assume you're hallucinating. But it's real. This is a regular stop for the nomadic people on their trading journeys. Here, they water their camels and replenish their own water supplies. They get a big surprise when they discover you at the well.

The nomads help tend to your sunburn (you ran out of sunblock a while ago), offer you a small amount of food (too much would be bad for you), and take you with them to safety. You're safe at last. Yet, you can't help but wonder whether things might have been a bit more interesting if you had set off into the desert instead . . .

The end.

You stumble along the sand dune, sweating even though the night is cold. You're sure this is the right way, so you're determined to keep going. Your boots are filled with sand, and you keep sinking into the sand as you stumble and slip down the dune. Your progress is painfully slow.

Eventually, you realize that you can't carry on—but by this time, it's too late. You're in the middle of a sea of undulating sand, and your water is very low. Without any means of finding more water, you die.

The end.

Sand Dunes

- The sand dunes of the Sahara, called ergs or sand seas, stretch for hundreds of miles (kilometers) and can be more than 600 feet (180 m) high.

- The Saharan winds have rubbed the sand into tiny grains, so the sand is very fine which makes it very difficult to cross. Travelers avoid the Great Western and Great Eastern Ergs, between Beni Abbes in Algeria and Ghadamis in Libya.

- The Great Western and Great Eastern Ergs cover most of Algeria; the Selima Erg covers more than 1,737 square miles (4,500 sq km) in Libya; and the Erg Cherch stretches for nearly 620 miles (1000 km) across Mali and Algeria.

- Ergs are formed by winds sweeping sand into heaps. Some dunes have a gentle slope on the windward side, with a steep drop on the side opposite the wind. Seif dunes are parallel to the prevailing winds and have sharp ridge lines.

- During sandstorms, great quantities of sand can be moved, completely altering the landscape.

You find out fairly quickly that it isn't a good idea to get close to ostriches. They are big, can be aggressive, and have very sharp claws on their feet that can kill a human. Added to this, they can run very fast—nearly 45 miles (70 km) per hour—so you definitely won't be able to outrun them.

These ostriches have young with them, so they're especially jumpy. A couple of the bigger birds trot away from the others toward you, watching you with what you imagine is an evil glint in their eyes. You remember hearing that birds such as these can be tricked into thinking you're bigger than you are if you raise your arms over your head. You raise your arms, but this seems to be the last straw for one of the ostriches. It sprints toward you.

The giant bird attacks by kicking out with its feet, which are armed with long, sharp claws. With one blow, you are dead.

The end.

Ostriches

- Ostriches are the largest birds on the planet—up to 9 feet (2.7 m) tall and 350 pounds (160 kg) in weight.

- They live in African savannahs and deserts, though they rarely stray into the Sahara Desert.

- Ostriches don't need to drink. They can get all the water they need from the plants they eat. They also eat insects and lizards.

- The birds can sprint up to 45 miles (70 km) per hour, keep up a speed of 30 miles (50 km) per hour over longer distances, and cover more than 16 feet (5 m) in just one stride.

- Ostriches live in small herds of about 10 birds. Their giant eggs weigh as much as 24 chicken eggs!

- These huge birds defend themselves from lions with their long claws, so it's not surprising that they are dangerous to humans. Ostriches kill a small number of people every year, but usually on ostrich farms. Like many animals, they're especially aggressive when they have young to defend.

You cut open the fruit with your knife. Inside there's greenish-white pulp and dark seeds. It looks quite appetizing, and you tentatively take a small bite. Blech! You spit the pulp and seeds out quickly—it tastes awful! The bitter taste makes you thirsty. You take a swig from your water bottle and spit it out before swallowing some, in case the fruit is poisonous.

In fact, this fruit is a desert gourd, which isn't poisonous, just foul-tasting. But you were taking a big chance by eating a fruit when you didn't know what it was. What were you thinking? You've had a lucky escape.

You decide to look for another water source.

Go to page 72.

Desert Gourds

- The desert gourd is a member of the watermelon family. It produces a vine that creeps across the desert floor, each one up to three yards (2.7 m) long. It has round fruits the size of an orange, which are yellow when ripe.

- The plant is quite common in the Sahara, as well as in desert-like conditions in many Arab countries, coastal India, and parts of the Mediterranean. It will grow in the hottest climates.

- Although the pulp is bitter and shouldn't be eaten, the succulent stems of the wild desert gourd can be used as an emergency water source. They can be chewed for their moisture.

- The seeds of the fruit are also edible—they're best roasted—and are rich in oil. The flowers can be eaten, too.

You start digging your hole for the solar still with your spade. The ground is hard, so it's tough work. You need to drink several times while you're digging. You hope that the water produced by the still is going to be enough. You wait all day, sheltering from the intense desert heat, while the still produces some fresh drinking water.

Unfortunately, it doesn't produce very much water at all—less than a pint (half a liter). It's not enough to keep you going. You're already dehydrated when you set off again at dusk. You don't find another water source in time to save you.

The end.

Making a Solar Still

- Dig a hole in the ground about three feet (90 cm) across and one and a half feet (45 cm) deep. If you can find any green leaves and grasses, put some in the hole.

- Put your container in the center of the hole, then cover the hole with a sheet of plastic, weighted down with a stone in the center above the container.

- Anchor your plastic sheet in place with sand or rocks.

- As the sun heats the air inside the hole, water vapor is produced, which condenses on the plastic and runs down into the container. Green plants will help make more water vapor.

- You can also use a solar still to distill water, or to make undrinkable water, such as seawater, pure. Put the salty or contaminated water in a larger container at the bottom of the hole, with a collecting can in the middle as before.

- Beware: a solar still can also act as a trap for snakes and creepy-crawlies, which might be able to get in…but not get out again.

You need water to replenish your supplies. You know how to make a solar still, although that would mean setting it up and waiting during the day. Or you could just keep walking and hope that you find another water source.

If you decide to make a solar still, go to page 70.

If you decide to look for another water source, go to page 52.

You hate retracing your steps, but you think it's important to wash the wound, which is painful and angry-looking. You're grateful for the bright moonlight as you find the well again and draw up some water to wash your wound. You even find a forgotten tube of antiseptic cream at the bottom of your backpack.

As you set off again, keeping well away from any animals you spot, you notice that there are a few clouds in the sky. The moon is still shining but, every so often, a cloud moves in front of it making it very difficult to see where you're going.

Go to page 84.

You slow down to a walk. You're sure this was the right thing to do—sweating makes your body lose salt as well as water, and not having enough of either can result in death. You're not sure where you're going anyway, so getting there fast isn't going to make much difference.

You hear some strange barking and whooping noises coming from higher ground on your right. You think it sounds a bit like chimpanzees, even though you know that chimps don't live here. As you walk, the sounds get louder. It almost sounds like laughter! Suddenly you spot them—dark shapes among the rocks. It's a group of hyenas. What should you do?

If you decide to run away and hide, go to page 60.

If you decide to walk confidently past them, go to page 40.

The wind is stronger now. It grabs your scarf and almost snatches it away. You wrap it around your mouth and nose against the sandy air. You have to put up your hands to shield your eyes. It's difficult to see anyway, because the moon is behind clouds.

The wind is howling now. The sand begins to whirl, and soon you can hardly see anything at all. The sandstorm is getting worse. You have to take shelter somewhere fast.

If you decide to shelter behind some large rocks on higher ground, go to page 87.

If you decide to shelter beside a nearby dune on lower ground, go to page 42.

You jump down into the wadi bottom and walk along the dry stream bed, which is rapidly turning to mud as the rain becomes heavier. You start to become alarmed at how quickly the thirsty ground has become thick, sucking mud . . . and you realize that this is a bad place to walk in a heavy downpour. You need to get out of the water and into some kind of shelter—fast!

You make for the side of the wadi but, as you do so, there's a roaring sound. Suddenly a huge torrent of water comes rushing around a bend in the dry river bed, sweeping you off your feet like a tsunami. Every time you come up gasping for air, the swirling water drags you down again. Half-drowned, you are bashed against a large rock.

The end.

Flash Floods

You might not have thought you would end up being swept away by a flood in the middle of a desert, but flash floods are one of the greatest perils of deserts around the world.

- Storms in deserts don't happen very often but, when they do, they can release a huge amount of rain very quickly.

- Flash floods can happen without warning. The storm that feeds the flood could be miles away.

- Be especially careful in canyons, which can channel water like a giant waterslide.

- Each year on average, flash floods are responsible for more deaths in the United States than hurricanes.

You struggle in the horrible, thick quicksand but it only makes you sink farther. The backpack is heavy and the bottom of it is already getting wet. You're very cold and wet, and now you're really starting to panic.

Then you have an idea: what if you spread your weight more evenly across the surface? You lean to the side and bring your legs up. You reach out toward the edge of the quicksand—you can now see the difference in color of the dry ground—all the while trying to keep the backpack out of the sand as much as possible. You're floating! It's quite easy to move to the side, even with your heavy backpack weighing you down.

You haul yourself out of the quicksand, quickly fling off your wet clothes and wrap yourself in the blanket, jogging on the spot to keep warm. When you're fairly dry, you step carefully around the quicksand to get water from the well.

With your bottles full of precious water, you set off. A cloud scuds across the moon, dimming your view of the desert. Then another. The wind starts to pick up. You can hear it howling as it scours the dry earth.

Go to page 75.

Quicksand

The best plan would be to take off your heavy backpack. Quicksand isn't as dangerous as you might have seen in the movies.

- Quicksand is simply very wet sand, clay, or silt. It can't suck you down (despite the myths about bottomless pits of doom).

- It looks just like ordinary sand, apart from the difference in color if the surrounding sand is dry, so it's easy to wander into it by accident.

- It's quite rare for quicksand to be deep enough that you can't reach the bottom.

- If you find yourself in quicksand, remove heavy objects and float across the surface to the side. Don't remain upright.

- Quicksand is usually made by underground springs pushing water upward into sand or silt. Here, it is created by the spring that feeds the well.

As you lick your parched lips, you realize that your enormous effort has made you incredibly thirsty. You should have slowed down well before now. In the desert, your main priority should be making sure you have enough water for the amount of work you're doing. Although you filled up at the wadi, you already drank most of it. You die of dehydration in a few days.

The end.

Keeping Hydrated

- If you live in a temperate climate, you will probably be surprised at how quickly you can become dehydrated in a desert. Check the chart on page 119 to see how much water you need.

- If you're lost in the desert, don't walk during the day because you don't know where your next water source might be.

- Don't run at any time, unless you absolutely have to (if, for example, you're being pursued by an angry baboon).

- We lose the most water from sweating. If you're very hot and suddenly stop sweating, you have heatstroke and need medical attention immediately.

- During the Second World War, the U.S. Army had a theory that soldiers could be trained to survive with less water, by gradually reducing their water supplies each day. It didn't work. Instead, it resulted in hundreds of sick, dehydrated soldiers.

- Don't eat, because water is used up in digesting food. You need water for cooling you down more than you need the food.

- Don't rely on thirst as a guide to your water requirements. Remember that the early stages of dehydration don't have any symptoms, and even mild dehydration can limit how well your body works.

- Dehydration also reduces concentration and alertness, which you're probably going to need in a survival situation.

- If your urine is dark colored, you're already dehydrated and you need to drink.

You head for the rocks in the half-light. As you climb them, the sun starts to sink over the horizon and the sky darkens even more.

You decide to climb as high as you can to get a good view before the light goes completely. However, this close to the equator, there isn't much of a twilight—darkness falls quickly, taking you by surprise. You've made a big mistake in climbing up here, especially without any kind of climbing gear or safety equipment.

You didn't really think this one through, did you? You get a fantastic view of the setting sun, but as darkness descends, you slip on some loose rocks and fall to your death. Look on the bright side: at least your last memory is of a beautiful sunset.

The end.

You find some rocks that look as though they might be a good place to rest during the day. You look around, trying to figure out the best place to lay your blanket where it will be shielded from the sun, when suddenly you are faced with one of the most hideous-looking creatures you have ever seen.

It looks like some sort of weird spider, hairy and about four inches (10 cm) long, with a huge head and frightening, over-sized jaws. Surely something this horrible has got to be venomous? It scuttles away from you at a surprising speed—faster than any spider—making you shudder.

If you decide to stay at these rocks, but keep away from the nasty-looking creature, which is obviously afraid of you, go to page 100.

If you decide to run away and find somewhere else to rest for the day, go to page 113.

The moon slips behind a cloud. You feel that there's a change in the air. The cold night feels slightly warmer. You sniff the air and detect a dampness to it. Surely it's not going to rain in the Sahara Desert? If it is, then maybe finding water wasn't such a necessity after all.

The first fat drops of rain begin to fall. There's a wadi, or dry river bed, not far away, which looks nice and flat and easy to walk along. Or should you climb a little higher so you can walk along the lower slopes of a mountainside to your right?

If you decide to walk along the high ground, go to page 88.

If you decide to walk along the wadi, go to page 76.

Rain in the Desert

- You might have thought that the whole point about deserts is the lack of rain. It is true that a desert is defined by its low annual precipitation of less than 10 inches (250 mm). But deserts—even the Sahara—do get some rain.

- Knowing the "average' rainfall isn't very useful if you want to know whether it's likely to rain in a desert, because the amount of rainfall is so erratic from year to year. An area might have 15 inches (380 mm) of rainfall one year, 12 inches (305 mm) the next year, and none at all the following year. But the average is still below 10 inches (254 mm).

- The low rainfall means that plants and animals have had to adapt to the arid conditions (see page 27). The resurrection plant is one of the most incredible in its adaptation. When there is no rain, this plant blows across the desert like a tumbleweed—brown, dried out, and dead-looking. But if it finds water, it quickly absorbs it and unfurls its leaves. Then it waits for rain to fall. If it does, its seeds fall, germinate, and produce shoots on the wet ground in a matter of hours. The plant can remain in its dried-out state for 100 years and still come back to life when it finds water.

You wriggle out of the backpack and fling it to the side. It slips on the edge, and gradually falls back into the quicksand. It's floating on the surface, but you can see it's starting to sink. Oh no! With a great squelch, you lunge for it—and, to your surprise, you discover that you can float on the quicksand. You reach the backpack, push it up onto solid ground, then clamber out yourself.

You're cold and wet, so you dry yourself the best you can with your blanket. Taking care not to fall into the quicksand again, you get water from the well. Quicksand is not actually the swamp of deadly peril you imagined it was (see page 79).

Clouds are racing across the sky, dimming the light of the moon. The wind has started to pick up.

Go to page 75.

You shelter behind a large rock, your scarf over your face to protect your eyes, nose, and mouth. Sand whirls into the air in a choking cloud as the wind howls around you. All you can do is sit and wait with your eyes closed. Thankfully, it soon begins to die down. After half an hour, the storm has blown over. You return to flatter ground as quickly as you can, and resume walking.

Suddenly you hear a loud barking sound—then a shriek. A rain of loose stones falls from some high rocks above you. Your heart pounding, you look up into the rocky hillside.

The moonlight reveals several big monkeys. Altogether you count 20 of them, and there might be more hiding in the rocks. A few of them are walking purposefully toward you. They have large, long, dog-like snouts. One of the bigger ones opens its mouth to reveal huge canine teeth. Maybe it's warning you away? Then again, they're only monkeys—how dangerous can they be?

If you decide to keep going past the baboons, go to page 90.

If you decide to back off and go a different way to avoid them, go to page 104.

The rain gets heavier quickly, drenching you. Soon it's a torrential downpour. It's difficult to see where you're going in the driving rain with the clouds hiding the moon, so you shelter by some rocks, amazed that you could be this cold and wet in the Sahara Desert.

After a while, the rain stops. The sky clears and you can now see where you're going. The rocks drip—and so do you! You pick up your pace to keep warm. As you hurry along, you look down to the wadi and see that it's completely flooded. It's just as well that you didn't take that route.

Go to page 98.

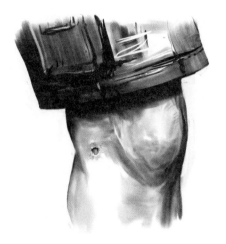

You're glad to have removed that creepy little creature. There's a small spot where it had buried into your skin, and you wash it with some of your water, just to be on the safe side.

As you walk on, you keep your eyes open for a new place to stock up on water.

Go to page 72.

As you pass closer to the baboon troop, they call to one another (or maybe to you), making loud, scary-sounding noises that sound like shrieks, screams, and barks. A few of them run toward you, then sit staring at you.

You're becoming more and more nervous. You pick up a large rock and chuck it at one of the baboons. That should scare them off.

It doesn't. Instead, the baboons return fire with rocks of their own, several of which hit you. Too late, you realize that the best thing to do around potentially dangerous wild animals is to remain calm and back off. Unfortunately, one of the largest male baboons attacks you. There are baby baboons in the troop, and he sees you as a threat—especially after you threw that rock.

The end.

Baboons

- There are five species of baboons, all native to Africa and Arabia. They are some of the largest monkeys in the world, with the biggest males weighing up to 80 pounds (37 kg) and measuring up to about three feet (1 m) tall.

- Baboons will eat almost anything: fruit, grass, seeds, and roots, but also meat—rodents, birds, and even the young of large mammals.

- Baboons form large groups called troops. There might be hundreds in a very large troop.

- They communicate with one another using a variety of different calls with different meanings.

- Baboons can be aggressive and have been known to hurt humans—but you were very unlucky to be killed.

It's not dark yet, but the sun is beginning to sink and the temperature has dropped, so you decide to get up and get moving.

You could head for higher ground, up some quite steep rocks, to get a good view of your surroundings. Or you could keep walking along the stone-covered, flat ground.

If you decide to take the higher ground, go to page 82.

If you decide to walk along the flatter ground, go to page 109.

As you get closer, you can see that the animals are definitely ostriches. There are 10 of them, you think. They're only a short distance away from you.

You are pretty sure that ostriches never roam too far from water. Should you approach them so that you can find their water source? Or do you worry that the ostriches could be dangerous?

If you decide to get closer to the ostriches, go to page 66.

If you decide to find water somewhere else, go to page 105.

You walk toward the shimmering water, but it doesn't seem to be getting any closer. After an hour or so of walking, you're burning hot and your water supplies are dangerously low. You hope you get to the sparkling lake soon.

Unfortunately, you never arrive because there's no water there at all—it's an illusion created by the hot sun on the desert sand. After a while, you're out of water and can't find any means of finding more.

The end.

Mirages

- Sometimes the heat of the desert will produce a layer of cooler air lying on top of a much hotter layer (or the other way around). Sunlight is refracted (bent) differently, resulting in an optical illusion: two images appear. An area of sky might be repeated below it on the desert sand, resembling a lake.

- A patch of sky repeated on the desert floor is called an inferior mirage, because it's underneath the true image. Some mirages are called superior mirages if the second image appears above the true one. So you might see a camel in mid-air above a camel on the ground!

- Mirages aren't hallucinations brought on by extreme thirst, as they're sometimes portrayed. They can actually be captured on camera. They are optical illusions, where the brain gets the wrong idea from the information taken in by the eye.

You set off after the camels in the breaking dawn, but they're too quick for you. Before long, they are too far away for you to bother chasing them anymore.

It's getting light, and soon it will be hot. Should you find somewhere to rest for the day, or carry on—at least for a while—and hope that you find rescue soon?

If you decide to rest, go to page 83.

If you decide to keep going, go to page 112.

Camels

- A Bactrian (or Asian) camel has two humps; a dromedary (or Arabian camel) has one. The humps don't store water, they contain fat. By keeping most of their fat in one place, camels can keep cooler. If you see a camel with a very floppy hump, it's probably a hungry camel, having used up all the hump's fat.

- Camels spit when they are angry. They have four separate chambers in their stomachs and can regurgitate (bring up) undigested food. They will spit it at whatever is bothering them.

- Camels are specially adapted to desert conditions:

  » They have extra long, curly eyelashes to keep sand out, and an extra eyelid to wipe it away.

  » They don't pant and hardly sweat; the moisture they breathe out is recycled because it trickles down a groove below their nostril and back into their mouth. They can also close their nostrils between breaths to keep out sand.

  » They have large soft pads on their feet that are specially adapted for traveling on sand.

  » Their droppings contain hardly any water. When they're fresh, the droppings are already dry enough to burn on a fire. In fact, people use camel dung as fuel.

- All these adaptations mean that a camel can travel 100 miles (160 km) in the desert without water. When it does find water to drink, a camel might drink 35 gallons (135 L) of water in less than 15 minutes.

A cascade of pebbles skitters down the rocks in front of you. You look up: there's a group of seven or eight sheep or goats up there. They have big, curled horns, shaggy manes, and hairy legs. They are staring at you in the moonlight. They're quite large, and each animal looks as though it is balanced precariously on the side of the cliff.

It clearly looks as though these animals live on this mountain, which means they must have some access to water. If you climbed up after them, maybe you'd find pools of water among the higher rocks. If so, this could be a good place to make a camp and wait to be rescued.

If you decide to climb up the mountain after the animals, go to page 106

If you decide to ignore the sheep and keep walking along the lower slopes, go to page 110.

It's already very hot now, and you realize that it's going to get hotter as the sun climbs higher in the sky. To the east, a wide stretch of blue shimmers in the distance. Could it be water sparkling in the sun? Maybe it's an oasis?

If you decide to go and investigate, go to page 94.

If you decide to keep going the way you're heading, go to page 103.

You lay your blanket down in a spot that will be shaded when the sun comes up, and sit down to take a drink. You reach for your backpack, and just as you're about to put your hand on the fastener, the hideous-looking spider creature scuttles across it! You jerk your hand back and lurch away from it, letting out a little scream.

Shivering with revulsion, you decide that there must be a number of these creatures here, and those jaws could probably give you a very nasty bite, whether they're venomous or not. You decide to make your bed for the day somewhere else.

Go to page 113.

Solpugids

- Although these creatures are sometimes called camel spiders, sun spiders, or wind spiders, they're not true spiders at all. They're actually solpugids, which are arachnids, like spiders and scorpions, but they're not quite the same as either creature.

- They have a huge head and jaws. In fact, they have the biggest jaws in relation to their size of any creature on Earth.

- There are lots of myths about solpugids, probably because they are so creepy to look at. Some of these myths are that they chase people and can run at incredible speeds (they do run very fast, up to 10 miles (16 km) per hour, but not faster than you!); that they eat people (and camels) alive while they're asleep; and that they have extremely powerful venom. Thankfully, none of them is true and, in fact, they're not venomous.

- Camel spiders are about six inches (15 cm) long (although there are myths that they're much bigger).

You start digging at the outside bend of the dry stream bed. The ground is hard and you start to sweat. You're very glad that it's not too hot yet, though it's getting hotter all the time as the sun climbs higher.

You haven't dug very deep when your spade makes a squelching noise. Thank goodness! You dig deeper and the hole fills with water. You rest in the shade of a boulder and boil the water (just to be on the safe side), then fill your bottles.

It won't be long before it's too hot to continue walking.

Go to page 99.

You're getting very hot and decide to stop and rest for the day. There's some high ground to one side of you, which you've been following for a while, where there are plenty of big rocks to offer shade. You make yourself comfortable and wait out the rest of the hot day, wondering if you're ever going to get out of the desert alive.

At long last, the sun starts to sink. You gather up your blanket and belongings and start walking. The rocks where you've been sheltering slope down to ground level just ahead of you. On the other side of them, you notice a flash of green. It looks as though there are some trees on the other side of the rocks— and what look like buildings, too. Maybe you've been waiting the whole day only an hour's walk from an oasis!

Go to page 114.

You carefully back off, glancing up every now and again at the monkeys, mindful not to make eye contact in case they see it as a threat. One of the males comes toward you, then sits on a rock, staring.

You were right to be wary of the monkeys. These are baboons, which can sometimes be dangerous to people.

When you're about 55 yards (50 m) or so away from them, you start to relax.

Go to page 84.

You need some water, but, since there's no obvious water source around, you'll need to dig. Now's the time to do it, before it gets really hot. If you leave it until later, you might end up becoming dehydrated before you've found enough water.

You can see some greenery in the distance. It could be some sort of tree. You can also make out a dry stream bed in the opposite direction. Where should you choose to dig?

If you decide to dig at the tree, go to page 111.

If you decide to dig at the stream, go to page 102.

The sheep—or goats, it's difficult to tell—are facing your way, munching the scraggly grass and leaves that grow on the mountainside. It's going to be a bit tricky, but the moon is bright, and you're confident of your climbing abilities.

You clamber up the rocks to a small ledge. As you straighten up, the animals above you suddenly turn and run off up the mountain, skittering across the rocks so fast you can hardly tell which way they went. Unfortunately, they've dislodged several large rocks, which bounce down the mountainside, knocking you off your feet and down to your death.

The end.

Barbary Sheep

- Barbary sheep are sandy colored, with a shaggy mane and hairy legs. They weigh up to 320 pounds (145 kg) and can measure more than three feet (1 m) tall.

- They live in mountainous areas and are extremely agile on steep rocks. They can jump up to six feet (2 m) high from a standing start. In their mountain environment, they're safe from predators.

- Barbary sheep are mostly crepuscular, which means they are active at dawn and dusk. They do this to avoid the heat of the day.

- They get all their moisture from the plants they eat, and don't need to drink at all. But if there's water available, they'll drink and wallow in it.

- Barbary sheep aren't aggressive and run away at the first sign of danger.

Y ou're pretty sure that following those camels would have been pointless. After all, they're much better equipped for moving in the desert than you are, and much faster, too.

The sky is getting lighter. As you walk, the sun comes up. The desert looks beautiful bathed in the dawn light. But that beautiful light can be deadly, too. You wonder how long it will be before you find an oasis and people to help you. Or whether you ever will.

You decide to look on the bright side: you're feeling OK, and you have plenty of water. So you decide to keep walking, at least for a while, until the heat becomes too intense.

Go to page 99.

The light is fading, and you know it won't be long until it's gone completely. You hope for another bright, moonlit night.

From the corner of your eye, you spot movement. Far in the distance, just emerging from behind a low hill, there's a camel. Squinting at it, you think you can make out the outline of a person riding it. Behind the camel, there's another one—and another one following that. They're walking in a line, one behind the other. It must be a camel train!

You call out, as loudly as you can. But even to you, your voice sounds feeble. You know it won't reach the camel riders. Still, you hope, maybe they're not far away from their destination—perhaps they're late getting back.

You hurry onward, following the direction of the camels.

Go to page 114.

You haven't gone far when you spot a different kind of creature in the distance: camels.

They're loping along the barren ground. You are disappointed to see there aren't any people with them.

Still, maybe you should follow them. You guess they'll eventually lead you to water.

If you decide to follow the camels, go to page 96.

If you decide not to, go to page 108.

As you get closer, you see that it's a single tree, about 15 feet (4.5 m) high, standing alone in parched-looking soil. It has small, green leaves, and it's covered in long, vicious-looking spines. But you're not interested in eating its leaves or climbing it—just in the water it must be drinking.

In fact the tree is an acacia tree, also known as a thorn tree. Its sharp thorns protect it from grazing animals. An acacia's roots can extend far underground to find water to sustain it.

You start to dig in the hard, parched earth. With every shovelful of soil, you hope to see water trickling into the hole, but the earth is dry.

You're sweating a lot, and you drank the last of your water. You have no choice but to carry on digging. Soon you're completely exhausted and dehydrated. With no other source of water and no energy to carry on digging, you soon die.

The end.

The sun isn't yet over the horizon, and it's still cool. You walk steadily, without any idea of where you're heading. You hope you'll spot something that might help you find other people soon.

Suddenly, you do spot something: a movement by some rocks in the distance. In the half-light, you can't make out what it is. Maybe animals . . . maybe people.

If you decide to go and investigate, go to page 93.

If you decide not to, go to page 105.

Y ou don't have to go far to find some more large
rocks to give you shelter from the sun. You carry
out a careful inspection to make sure there aren't
any more creatures like that scary thing you just saw.
(It was a solpugid—see page 101.) After a thorough
investigation, you're satisfied that there aren't any,
and you can't see any snakes, scorpions, or other
creepy-crawlies either.

You spread your blanket on the ground and put your backpack
down. Before you lie down, you have an idea: you gather a big
pile of stones and spell out SOS in huge letters on the desert
floor. You never know—a passing helicopter might spot them.
It's heavy work and, by the time you finish, the sun is starting
to go down.

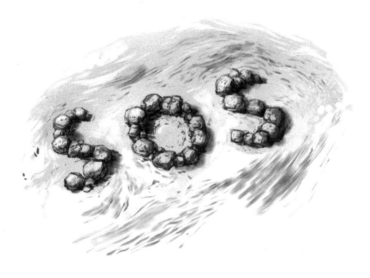

Go to page 92.

As you follow the camel train, it leads you to an oasis. Its lights twinkle in the darkness—that means people! Palm trees sway in a gentle breeze. It's the most welcome sight you've ever seen!

You're almost crying with relief as you get closer. You call out, and two people come running. They offer shelter, food, and water, and promise to get you back to your friends and family the next day.

Soon you're home. You've survived your amazing Saharan adventure!

The end.

Oases

- An oasis is a fertile area in a desert, fed by a source of fresh water. It might be just a few palm trees around a well, or it could be much bigger. For example, the Kharga Oasis in Egypt is 100 miles (160 km) long and has a population of more than 100,000.

- Underground water sources called aquifers supply most oases. The water might come up to the surface naturally from an underground spring, or people might dig wells to get to the aquifer.

- Palms are planted all around oases to keep out the desert sands. People also plant crops, such as dates (which grow on certain types of palm trees), olives, figs, oranges, lemons, and cotton.

- The Nile River is the only permanent river in the Sahara. The rest of the region's water lies in underground aquifers.

- There are about 90 major oases in the Sahara, but traveling between them might take days.

The People of the Sahara Desert

People are totally dependent on water for survival, so permanent homes in the Sahara are limited to oases, and the towns and cities on the edges of the desert. But some people who live in the Sahara don't have permanent homes: nomadic people spend some of the year traveling through the desert and the rest in the mountains or at an oasis.

Nomads live by herding camels, sheep, and goats, and trading between oases and cities on the edge of the desert. Salt is important for trade because it's in short supply in the Sahara. For hundreds of years, the Tuareg nomads have transported salt on camel trains. In Niger, they still do—the Tuareg cross the desert to the Bilma oasis, then transport the salt, packed into cakes or cone shapes, for trade elsewhere. In the past, they traded in gold and spices, too. Today, there are about a million Tuareg people in and around the Sahara. Some of them still lead a nomadic lifestyle, while others have settled in towns and cities.

Sahara Mountains

There are several mountain ranges within the Sahara Desert. The Air Mountains in northern Niger rise to nearly 6,000 feet (1,800 m) and cover more than 32,000 square miles (82,000 sq km). Mount Emi Koussi, in the Tibesti Mountains of northern Chad, is the highest peak in the Sahara at 11,204 feet (3,415 m) high. The Tassili n'Ajjer mountain range in Algeria covers 28,000 square miles (72,000 sq km) and is famous for its prehistoric rock art, which reveals that the Sahara once had a very different climate: hippos and crocodiles lived here during the Stone Age.

Expanding Sahara

The Sahel borders the Sahara Desert to the south. It is a semi-arid belt of grassland that supports semi-nomadic people who farm and raise livestock. Changing patterns of rainfall, clearing land for fuel, and intensive farming have led to the spread of the desert. Areas that were once green and forested are now dry and lifeless.

Other Deserts

Deserts are places where there is very little precipitation. While all of them are dry, not all of them are hot. The Antarctic is the largest desert in the world—more than one and a half times the size of the Sahara. It receives an average of eight inches (200 mm) of precipitation per year in its coastal regions, less inland. It's the coldest place on Earth: the temperature plummets to as low as -128°F (-89°C).

Deserts take up around a third of Earth's land surface. Other deserts around the world include the following:

- The Gobi Desert stretches for nearly 502,000 square miles (1.3 million sq km) across China and Mongolia. It's a cold desert, though temperatures in some areas can reach 95°F (35°C). Like the Sahara, it has vast sand dunes, but most of the Gobi Desert is bare rock.

- The Atacama Desert in Chile is high above sea level and is the driest place on Earth after Antarctica. In some parts of the desert, rainfall has never been recorded, and the desert is completely barren there.

- The Mojave Desert in North America spans California, Nevada, and Utah. It includes one of the most famously hot and inhospitable places on Earth—Death Valley—where the temperature can reach 129°F (54°C) in summer.

- The Namib Desert in southern Africa stretches for 1,242 miles (2,000 km) along the coasts of Angola, Namibia, and South Africa. It has vast sand dunes near the coast. The largest dunes are 985 feet (300 m) high and 19 miles (30 km) long.

How much water do you need to drink?

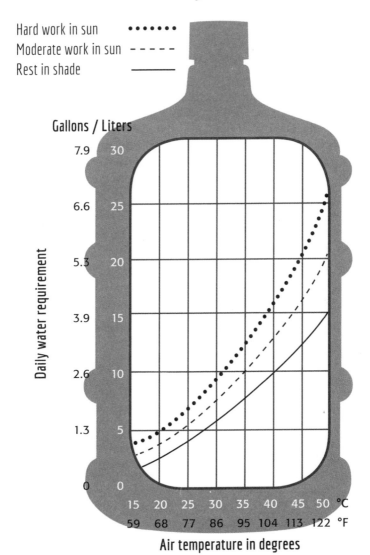

Hard work in sun **••••••**
Moderate work in sun **– – – –**
Rest in shade **————**

Gallons / Liters

Daily water requirement

Gallons	Liters
7.9	30
6.6	25
5.3	20
3.9	15
2.6	10
1.3	5
0	0

°C	15	20	25	30	35	40	45	50
°F	59	68	77	86	95	104	113	122

Air temperature in degrees

This water chart is only an approximate guide. Seek out expert advice for more detailed information.

Real-life Lost-in-the-Desert Stories

People really have ended up lost in the Sahara Desert. Not all of them have lived to tell the tale.

The Marathon des Sables (Marathon of the Sands) is an extreme 156-mile (251 km) marathon run across the Sahara Desert in Morocco over six days. It's a grueling race, considered to be the most difficult foot race in the world. Mauro Prosperi, an Italian policeman, was competing in the 1994 Marathon des Sables, when a sandstorm blew up. In the swirling sand, he was unable to see and became completely lost. Mauro didn't have any water on him at all, and yet he survived for nine days. He drank his own urine (which is absolutely NOT recommended!), and ate snakes, scorpions, lizards, and some bats that he discovered while sheltering in an abandoned Muslim shrine. He wasn't lucky enough to come across any wells or water holes, so it's incredible that he survived. Eventually, he met a nomad family who helped him return to safety. He had wandered 125 miles (200 km) away from the course of the marathon. Mauro made a complete recovery and, surprisingly, he has since completed the Marathon des Sables many times.

According to Ancient Greek historian Herodotus, an entire Persian army got lost in the Sahara Desert and never found their way out. In 525 BCE, the army of 50,000 soldiers was sent into the Sahara by the King of Persia, Cambyses II. Halfway across the desert, heading for the remote Siwa Oasis in Egypt, an immense sandstorm blew up. Not one of the men ever made it to the oasis. People have been looking for their remains ever since.

Glossary

adobe A natural building material made of sand, clay, and water

amoebas Small organisms made of only one cell

antibiotics Medicines that kill bacteria

aquifer An underground water source

Arabia A peninsula in southwest Asia bordered by the Red Sea, the Persian Gulf, and the Indian Ocean. The area includes Saudi Arabia, Yemen, Lebanon, and Iraq, among other countries.

arid Dry; lacking a water source

carrion Dead animals

contaminated Unclean

crepuscular Active at dawn and dusk

disoriented Confused, lost

dysentery An infection causing diarrhea

epidemics Diseases affecting large numbers of people at once

ergs Sand dunes

escarpment A steep slope or cliff

flash flood Sudden, quick flooding caused by very heavy rain

germinate To begin to grow and develop

hallucinations Things you can see that do not really exist

hamadas Desert landscapes consisting of high, exposed rock

hemisphere Half of Earth

hyponatremia A lack of salt in the blood

metabolic rate The amount of energy used

mirage An optical illusion caused by light rays bending to produce an image such as water

nomads People who do not have one permanent home but move from one place to another

oases Isolated areas of vegetation in deserts

parasite A creature that lives by attaching itself to and feeding on another creature

plains Broad expanses of flat land

proximity How close something is

refracted Light or other waves being bent

regs Rocky plains

regurgitate Bring swallowed food out of the mouth

scavengers Animals that feed on dead animals or plants

sepsis Blood poisoning

serrated Having a notched or saw-like edge

silt A grainy material that is a bit thicker than sand

succulent Juicy, water-storing

tick A small parasite that lives on the blood of other creatures

venomous Capable of injecting venom

wadi Arabic word for dry river bed or dry valley

Learning More

Alloway, David. *Desert Survival Skills*. University of Texas Press, 2000.

Aloian, Molly. *The Sahara Desert*. (Deserts Around the World) Crabtree Publishing Company, 2012.

Bowles, Paul. *The Sheltering Sky*. Ecco, 2005.

Dowswell, Paul. *True Desert Adventure Stories*. Usborne Publishing Ltd., 2002.

Harvey, Gill. *Desert Adventures* (Usborne True Stories). Usborne Publishing Ltd., 2008.

McCaughrean, Geraldine. *One Thousand And One Arabian Nights*. Oxford University Press, 2000.

Raskin, Lawrie, and Debora Pearson. *52 Days by Camel: My Sahara Adventure*. Annick Press, 2008.

White, Robb. *Deathwatch*. Laurel Leaf, 1973.

Websites

Africa: Explore the Regions (Sahara)
www.pbs.org/wnet/africa/explore/sahara/sahara_overview_lo.html

The Sahara: Facts, Climate and Animals of the Desert
www.livescience.com/23140-sahara-desert.html

Expansion of the Sahara (BBC)
www.bbc.co.uk/learningzone/clips/desertification-expansion-of-the-sahara-desert/1498.html

A Kid's Wilderness Survival Primer (Equipped to Survive Foundation)
www.equipped.org/kidprimr.htm

List of great books about survival (Indianapolis Public Library)
www.imcpl.org/kids/blog/?page_id=12516

Survival Tips (I Shouldn't Be Alive—Animal Planet)
www.animalplanet.com/tv-shows/i-shouldnt-be-alive/videos/survival-tips-videos.htm

Desert Survival Skills
www.desertusa.com/desert-activity/desert-survival-skills.html

Index

acacia trees 9, 111
amoebas 46
antelopes 9, 27, 52
antiseptic cream 47, 73
aquifers 115

baboons 8, 81, 87, 90–91, 104
backpacks 7, 11, 12, 26, 30, 38,
   47, 62–62, 73, 78–79, 86,
   100, 113
bacteria 14, 46, 49, 53, 56
Bactrian camels 97
baobab trees 9, 27, 55
Barbary sheep 9, 98, 106–107
blood poisoning 14
buildings 21–22, 30, 48, 103

cactuses 55
camel spiders 101
camel train 63, 109, 116
camels 7, 9, 27, 63, 95–97, 101,
   108–110, 116
canyons 77
carrion 15
cats 34, 53, 58–59
caves 13, 18, 31, 51
clouds 73, 75, 78, 84, 86–88
compasses 37
crepuscular animals 15, 107

deathstalker scorpions 8, 18–19
dehydration 16, 70, 80–81,
   105, 111
desert gourds 55, 68–69
desert plants 27, 54–55,
   68–69, 85
directions, finding 36–37, 39
dromedary camels 97
dysentery 46–47

ergs 8, 65

farming 117
fire 14, 21, 28–29, 50, 52, 97
flash floods 23, 77
flies 49, 57
fruits 15, 27, 54–55, 68–69, 91
fuel 29, 97, 117

gazelles 14, 15

hamadas 8
heatstroke 10, 16, 81
hunting 15, 20, 32, 41, 59
hyenas 8, 40–41, 74
hyponatremia 24–25, 63

jackals 8, 14–15, 21
jerboas 9, 59, 63
jogging 38, 45, 78

lizards 15, 20, 27, 33, 59, 63,
   67, 120

malaria 57
Marathon des Sables 120
matches 11, 14, 29
metabolic rate 19
mirages 94–95, 99
monkeys, see baboons
mosquitoes 49, 57
mountains 8–9, 84, 98,
   106–107, 116–117

Nile River 8, 115
nocturnal animals 19, 27, 33
nomads 9, 63, 116, 120

oases 8, 9, 99, 103, 108,
   114–115, 116, 120
ostriches 8, 66–67, 93

palm trees 62, 114–115
plains 8

quicksand 62, 78–79, 86

rainfall/precipitation 9, 76,
    84–85, 88, 117, 118
regs 8
relapsing fever 56–57
rescue 10, 11, 30, 48, 96, 113
resurrection plant 85
river beds 9, 23, 39, 76
rocks, climbing 82, 98, 106

salt 10, 24–25, 30, 46, 63, 74,
    116
sand cats 34, 53, 58–59
sand dunes 8, 17, 20, 42–44,
    64–65, 75, 118, 119
sand vipers 20
sandstorms 7, 42–43, 65, 75,
    87, 120
saw-scaled vipers 32–33
scorpions 8–9, 13, 18–19, 33,
    101, 113, 120
sepsis 14
shade 11, 13, 16, 21, 22, 23, 30,
    51, 53, 100, 102, 103
shelters 11, 22–23, 35, 42–43,
    75–76, 87–88, 113–114
sleeping sickness 57
snakes 8–9, 13, 15, 20, 32–33,
    50, 71, 113, 120
solar stills 70–72
solpugids 100–101, 113
spiders 9, 19, 83, 100–101
stream beds 13, 76, 102, 105
sunburn 16, 24, 63
sweating 10, 12, 16, 23–27,
    30, 35, 38, 44, 64, 74, 81, 97,
    102, 111

temperature 9, 10, 11, 13,
    16, 21, 24, 30, 39, 48, 92,
    118–119

ticks 56, 60, 89
trade 9, 116
trenches 23, 29
tsetse flies 57

venomous animals, 9, 18–19,
    32–33, 50, 83, 100, 101
vultures 7, 27

wadis 8–9, 39, 76, 80, 84, 88
watch, using as a compass
    36–37
water
  boiling 11, 28, 46, 49, 52, 102
  conserving 10, 27
  consumption 10, 21, 25, 27,
    30, 48, 52, 59, 63, 67, 70,
    81, 97, 100, 102, 119
  filtering 49
  holes 28, 49, 50, 120
  sources 11, 28, 48–49, 50, 53,
    68, 93, 105
wells 47–48, 62–63, 120
wind 7, 8, 29, 42, 43, 65, 75,
    78, 86, 87